THE MAGIC STONE

ANNE SCHRAFF

SCHOLASTIC INC.

Copyright © 2015 by Saddleback Educational Publishing.
All rights reserved. Published by Scholastic Inc., 557 Broadway, New York, NY 10012,
by arrangement with Saddleback Educational Publishing.
Printed in the U.S.A.

ISBN-13: 978-1-338-06057-7
ISBN-10: 1-338-06057-0

3 4 5 6 7 8 9 10   40   25 24 23 22 21 20 19 18

Ms. Nealy

Age: 84

Biggest Secret: she invented toe socks

Favorite Sport: baseball

Best Health Tip: don't eat sugar

Best Quality: she always has a positive attitude

CHARACTERS

KIRBY

Age: 10

Worst Habit: bites his nails

Least Favorite Food: bacon

Biggest Fear: that he hit his growth spurt too soon

Best Quality: he is a loyal friend

1
DON'T WALK

Kirby Aki headed to school. He crossed Madison Avenue every day. It was a busy road. The ten-year-old pushed the button. He waited for the Walk sign.

"Look both ways before crossing," said

his mom. Some drivers didn't stop for red lights. Even if the sign flashed "Walk." They drove very fast.

Today Kirby waited to cross. Just like always. A slim man stood beside him. Kirby had never seen him before. He was also waiting to cross. He was talking on his cell phone. He wore a red shirt. He spoke in a foreign language.

↖ VERY ANIMATED
ON THE PHONE!

The man stepped into the street. A big truck was coming fast. The light was yellow. But the truck didn't slow down. It sped up. Kirby wanted to scream. "Look out!" he would yell. But the man wouldn't understand. Would he? He wasn't speaking English.

Kirby panicked. He had to do something. The truck was coming. The man wasn't paying attention. He was still on his phone. So Kirby reached out. He grabbed the man.

Kirby was tall for his age. And strong too. He yanked the man backward. Both fell onto the sidewalk. The big truck sped by.

The man got up. He didn't seem hurt.

He helped Kirby stand up. The man looked stunned. Kirby couldn't speak.

An older woman saw what happened. She wore a Dodgers baseball cap. She always wore it. Kirby recognized her. She knew Kirby's mom.

SHE SAW THE WHOLE THING →

"Whoa! That was crazy," she said. "You both okay?"

The man was shaking. He stared at Kirby. "You saved me. You saved me," he said.

"I'm glad," Kirby said. He tried to smile. But he was shaking too.

"I would be dead now," the man cried. "You saved me!"

He reached into a cloth bag he carried. He took out a yellow stone. It was about the size of Kirby's palm.

"I don't have money for you, " he said. "But here. Take this. I thank you for my life. You take this. It's magic. You know magic?"

Kirby nodded. He knew about magic.

"Rub the stone. You will get your wish. Rub it, okay? It happens. I promise you. You rub, you wish. It happens. Here, take it. It will change your life. I promise you!"

2
AN OLD ROCK

Kirby didn't believe it. But he took the stone. It was beautiful. "Thank you," Kirby said.

"Thank *you*," the man said. "For my life!"

"You both go home," the woman said. "You are shook up."

They all crossed Madison. The woman went into a store. The man went right. He vanished into a crowd. Kirby shook his head. He put the stone in his pocket.

It all happened so fast. It was like a dream. The big truck was speeding. The man was talking. Not paying attention. He never saw the truck.

Kirby didn't have time to think. He felt good about what he did. He never did anything like that before. He never did anything so important.

Kirby wondered if it happened at all.
Then he reached in his pocket. There it was.
The yellow stone. Kirby pulled it out. He
looked at it. It was smooth.

Kirby liked rocks. On his vacations he
collected them. He liked rock collecting. But
they were just rocks. A magic one? No, that
was crazy. Still, the man said …

Kirby didn't believe it. He thought about
the man. Was he a wizard? Kirby wasn't
sure. The man did look different. He had
bright eyes. Shaggy hair. A beard. He wasn't

from around here. Still, his English was pretty good. He had a little accent.

This is just some old rock, Kirby thought. He laughed. *Magic stone? Nah.*

The man was thankful. Kirby had saved him. Maybe the pretty yellow stone was all he had. He made up the magic part. To make it sound more valuable.

"Rub the stone. You will get your wish. Rub it, okay? It happens. I promise you. You wish, you rub. It happens. Here, take it. It will change your life. I promise you!" the man had said.

Kirby laughed again. He put the stone in his backpack. He would keep it. He didn't believe it was magic. But it was cool. It would remind him of what happened today. Being a hero made him feel good.

Kirby walked home. He wondered about

the stone. What kind was it? Where did it come from?

Kirby's best friend was Jalen. Jalen had an uncle who knew stuff. He even knew about rocks. Would he know about this one? Kirby would show him.

Kirby had a funny thought. His favorite pie was mince. But Mom didn't make it often. It was a holiday treat. Wouldn't it be sweet if Mom made it today? Kirby took out the yellow stone. He rubbed it. *Here goes nothing*, he thought.

He imagined eating a piece. Yummy! So good. He wished for pie.

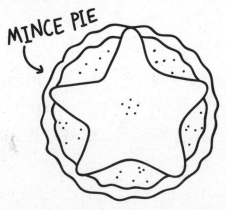

MINCE PIE

3
SO PROUD

Kirby couldn't wait to tell his parents. He'd saved a man. He got a yellow stone as a reward. But he wouldn't talk about the magic. Not yet. Mom and Dad might laugh.

Kirby's parents sold houses. Mom was always home early. Just before Kirby got there. But today both of his parents were home.

"Mom! Dad!" Kirby shouted. He threw down his backpack. "The most rad thing happened. Just now. I saved a man. He was almost hit by a truck."

"What?" Dad cried. "Tell us what happened, Kirby."

"Oh my goodness," Mom gasped. "I can't catch my breath."

OXYGEN

"Me and this man. We were waiting at the crosswalk. The one at Madison. I pushed the button. Waited for the Walk sign. The man was on his phone. He stepped off the curb. Before the Walk sign came on. This big truck was coming. It wasn't going to stop."

"Oh, Kirby," Dad groaned. "How awful! Madison is terrible. Drivers go too fast."

MADISON AVE

TERRIBLY FAST DRIVERS

"Yeah. I know. It's crazy-bad. I grabbed the man. Pulled him back on the sidewalk. Then the truck zoomed by. It never stopped. We both fell. But nobody got hurt."

"Kirby," Mom cried. "You're a hero!"

"Aw. Thanks, Mom."

Kirby got his backpack. He pulled out

the yellow stone. "The man spoke with an accent. He was thankful. He gave me this rock. I guess it was all he had."

"We are proud of you, son," Dad said. He gave Kirby a hug.

Mom hugged Kirby too. "Sweetie," she said. "I'm always proud of you. But this is remarkable!"

Kirby's father served in the army. That was years ago. He won some medals. Kirby was proud of his dad. But now Kirby felt like a hero too. He was proud. And happy. Nothing felt better than this. He'd saved someone's life.

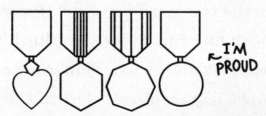

The man probably had a family. That

made Kirby feel great. He'd saved some kid's father!

Kirby would never forget. The man's red shirt. His shaggy hair. His bright black eyes. His beard. His look of gratitude. Today was special. It was one of the biggest in his life.

Kirby went to his room. He was still holding the yellow stone. The man probably wasn't rich. Most people weren't. Everyone worked hard. Did the best they could. Everyone wanted a happy life. To be free. And feel safe.

The man only had the yellow stone. It was pretty. Kirby would treasure it. It would remind him of today. But he knew it had no magic. He needed no reward.

It was dinnertime. He put the stone down. Sighed. He wished it were magic.

Then maybe there would be pie. Yummy pie. His favorite.

Dinner smelled great. Kirby went to the kitchen. Mom was making fried chicken.

"Honey, you've been hinting. I know you want mince pie. And this morning I made a pie. Mince! We're having it for dessert. I know it's not a big reward. But it *is* your favorite."

SURPRISE
↩ DESSERT!

Kirby turned numb. Mince pie? Tonight? He'd rubbed the stone. He'd wished for it! No way! It couldn't be …

4
OKAPI PROJECT

The pie was a home run. The best ever. His mother outdid herself. Why was he eating pie? Because of some rock? It had nothing to do with it. Kirby was sure. It was just a fluke. Besides, she'd made the pie that morning. Before the rescue.

COOKED TO PERFECTION

Kirby helped clean up. Then he put the

yellow stone in his dresser. He got ready for homework. There was a big school project due. He would do his work. Then go to bed.

STUFFED →
WITH
HOMEWORK

His teacher was Ms. Larimer. She was good. But she was hard. The project was about endangered animals. Each student had to pick one.

"Look on the Internet. Read books. Do research," Ms. Larimer said. "Then write a report. There will be an oral portion. And a media portion. You will need a good video."

Kirby was good at writing reports. Making speeches scared him. He got nervous. He stumbled over words. He was shy. Sometimes the kids laughed at his mistakes.

Lee Watkins was the worst. Lee was smart. He usually got the best grade. His parents were both teachers. They helped Lee a lot. He even bragged about it.

LEE WATKINS

The last report was hard. Kirby's was about auroras. Jalen's was about sunspots. Lee's was about Jupiter. It was the best

report. He made a video. He made a model
of Jupiter.

One girl said, "Wow, Lee. That report was
great."

Lee laughed. "Yeah. Thanks. My parents
were up all night. They put it together."

"We're supposed to do our own work,"
another girl snapped.

"And not the night before. That's lame,"
said a boy.

It was not fair. Kirby knew it. So did

some other kids. Lee was supposed to do his own work. But Kirby didn't say anything. He didn't need any trouble.

It was the next afternoon. Kirby and Jalen walked home from school.

"What animal did you pick, Kirby?" Jalen asked.

"Everybody wanted elephants. Or rhinos. I picked a rare animal. An okapi," Kirby said. "It's like a zebra. And it has stripes. It's the only relative of the giraffe."

OKAPI

"How come it's endangered?" Jalen asked.

"It lives in central Africa. In the Ituri Forest. People are cutting down the trees. They are making farms," Kirby said.

Kirby hadn't told Jalen about yesterday. About saving the man on Madison. Kirby didn't want it to get around school. Lee and his friends would tease him.

Lee would call Kirby a liar. Kirby was a nobody. Not a hero. Lee was a bully. He *would* say that.

Kirby's father did not talk about the

army. About what he went through. He put his medals away. Kirby figured heroes were like that.

Kirby got home. He did more research. About the okapi. About central Africa. He found some pictures. A video showed the okapi eating leaves. The white-and-black striped legs stood out. Kirby's laptop came in handy. He made a movie from all the images he found.

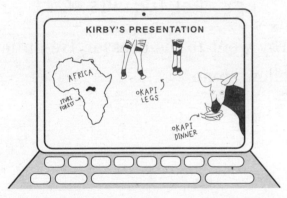

Kirby was feeling better about his report.

He had so much information. Plus he had a great video. Maybe he wouldn't get nervous. Not like he usually did.

Kirby dreaded losing his cool. He dreaded stammering in front of the class. Lee and his friends would giggle. Roll their eyes.

LEE, ROLLING HIS EYES

Kirby went to his dresser. He pulled out the yellow stone.

5
MAKE A WISH

Kirby's mom used to read him stories. He loved it when he was little. He was too old for stories now. Once, she read a story about a boy named Aladdin. He rubbed his magic lamp. He made good things happen. Just by wishing!

Kirby shrugged. That was how he remembered the story. *Wait. Wasn't there a genie? Yeah. Whatever.* He put the yellow stone away. It was silly. A rock couldn't help him with his project.

Instead, Kirby practiced his report. He looked in the mirror. He said the words. He slowly pronounced each one. He made sure he could say each word correctly. He did not want to stumble. Not tomorrow. It was too important.

Kirby worked until bedtime. He felt prepared. But he was still nervous.

In the morning, Kirby felt bad. He knew he would mess up his report. He would be a fourth-grade joke. Suddenly Kirby jerked open his dresser drawer. He didn't care if it was stupid. He grabbed the yellow stone. He rubbed it.

I HAVE NOTHING → TO LOSE!

He wanted to do well. He wished for it. He wanted his report to be good. He thought about what the man said. If he wanted to make something happen ... Rub the stone. And wish.

Kirby felt silly on his walk to school. He was prepared. He didn't need magic. Why couldn't he believe in himself?

The class was excited. It was report day. Ms. Larimer shushed her students.

Lee gave his report first. It was very good. Then a girl gave her report. She did well too.

Kirby was next. His legs felt weak. But he stood. And walked to the front of the room. His video was ready. He tried not to look at Lee.

I'M SO NERVOUS

THE OKAPI

By Kirby Aki

Kirby took a deep breath mysterious. They are sh discovered a century ago," K was surprised. He felt con didn't know what to call the okapi. They called it the forest donkey." Some kids laughed. But not in a bad way. They thought the forest donkey was a funny name.

Kirby's video was cool. And creative. He talked about how people loved the okapi. He talked about the rain forest. He talked

...he problems of central Africa. How
...d life was there. How so many helped to
save the animals.

Kirby ended his report. Ms. Larimer said, "Excellent, Kirby. Your best report ever."

Kirby felt proud. He felt happy too. But he wasn't sure. Was it good work? Or the stone's magic? That thought ruined it for him.

At lunchtime, Kirby told Jalen about saving the man. About the dangerous truck on Madison. He told Jalen to keep it a secret.

"Wow! You're a hero, dude," Jalen said.

"Nah, I just did what I had to do," Kirby said. "I wonder who the man was."

"What did he look like?" Jalen asked.

"He was short. Older. I don't know. Like my parents. His hair was bushy. He had a beard. Wore a red shirt. Jeans," Kirby said.

"Wait," Jalen said. "You said this happened on Madison?"

"Yeah," Kirby said.

"I've seen a dude like that," Jalen said. "There's a lot of Middle Eastern stores there. My mom likes a kind of pastry. It's called *awamat*. Like a doughnut hole," Jalen explained. He licked his lips. "Dude, it's *so* good. Anyway. She goes over there a lot. I've seen that short man. Always wears a red shirt. Has a beard. They call him Al. Don't know his last name. "

AWAMAT
(YUM!)

6
JUST A ROCK

"Al?" Kirby cried. "Like Aladdin!"

"Huh?" Jalen said.

"Yeah. Don't you remember? That old fairy tale 'Aladdin's Magic Lamp.' It's from *The Arabian Nights*. This boy, Aladdin, gets a magic lamp. When he rubs it, stuff happens. Good stuff. And the man I saved, his name is Al. Wow."

"Kirby? A genie lived in the lamp. You see any genies here? Huh?" Jalen asked. "Yo. What aren't you telling me?"

GENIE?

Kirby almost told Jalen about the yellow stone. But he stopped himself. Jalen would think Kirby was nuts. A rock that granted wishes? Who would believe that?

Kirby wanted to tell his friend. He tried to find a way. Jalen was his bud. He *had* to know about the yellow stone.

"You know, that man is probably poor. I

mean Al. Maybe he has a big family. He was thankful for what I did. He wanted to give me something. But not money. So he gave me a yellow stone. It's cool."

Jalen blinked. "He gave you a *rock*?"

"Yeah. But he said it was a special *stone*," Kirby said.

"Maybe it's a gem. Or something," Jalen said. "Maybe it's worth some money, dude. Why don't you let my uncle look at it? He always comes to Sunday dinner. Bring your stone over after dinner. See what he says."

Kirby shrugged. "Okay. But I think it's just a plain old rock."

The boys finished lunch. It was time for recess.

It was early Sunday afternoon. Kirby skateboarded to Jalen's house. He had his yellow stone. It felt heavy in his pocket. Kirby liked rocks. He had several boxes of them. Mostly colorful agates. This rock was probably worthless. That was the news he expected.

INSIDE CUT AGATE

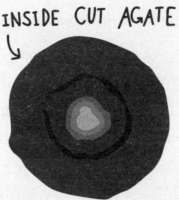

Kirby thought about the man in the red shirt. He wanted to give Kirby a reward. Kirby had been brave. The stone was all he had. So he gave it to Kirby. And he told him the silly story about magic.

Kirby knocked on the door. The family was in the living room. The adults were drinking coffee. Jalen was eating chocolate cake. Jalen's mom gave Kirby a slice too.

"Kirby, Jalen told us a story. He said you saved a man last week," Jalen's dad said. "You pulled him on the sidewalk. That truck could have killed him. That was brave. You'll remember it forever. And you should. You're a hero."

"Gosh. Thank you," Kirby said. He didn't know what else to say. He told Jalen's family about the stone. Kirby gave it to Jalen's uncle. He examined it.

"Let's see," Jalen's uncle said.

"The man gave me this. I guess he didn't have anything else. He looked poor. He wanted to give me something."

Jalen's uncle turned the rock over in his hand. "Well, I don't have to do a lot of tests. I know what this is. It's calcite. Calcite is a carbonate. It's very common. It's a fine example, though. Probably came from Michigan. Calcite is used in manufacturing."

It was just as Kirby thought. It was a plain old rock. It wasn't special. It wasn't worth anything. Kirby knew it. But he was still disappointed.

7
THE WATERFALL

Kirby skateboarded home. It was a nice afternoon. He took the long way.

Okay, I'm done with this old rock, Kirby thought. *Back in the drawer. I won't even think about it. It had nothing to do with anything. The pie? Mom was going to make it anyway. I was nagging her for weeks! My*

okapi project? I worked hard. Really hard! I studied like crazy. This is a worthless rock.

He passed a little stream. Part of it ran downhill. It would turn into a small waterfall after a rain. Kirby always liked looking at it. It had rained last night. The waterfall should be big.

An idea came to him. Maybe he should get rid of the stone. Toss it into the waterfall. It would vanish into the stream. Then he would be done with it. He wouldn't be tempted to rub it. He wouldn't expect magic.

Kirby reached into his pocket. He felt the rock. Not everything good came from it. He was tired of thinking it did.

Kirby reached the waterfall. It was beautiful. The water sparkled in the sunlight. A good place for the yellow stone. It was in his hand. He was ready to throw it. But then he heard a child crying.

A little girl. She was with her mother. She looked about six years old. Her cheeks were red. Her eyes watery. She was looking for something.

LITTLE GIRL TEARS
MAKE ME WANT TO CRY

Her mother was upset too. She turned to Kirby. "My little girl lost her necklace," she said. "It was from her dad. She loves it so much. It's somewhere in the grass."

The girl was rubbing her eyes. "Oh, Mommy," she said. "Please find my red necklace. Please!"

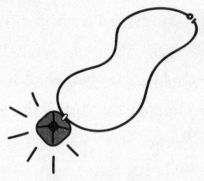

"Let me help you look," Kirby offered. "I'm pretty good at finding stuff."

Kirby walked slowly through the grass. He looked down. Was there anything sparkly? Anything red? But the grass was tall. And thick. There were pebbles. Leaves.

Twigs. Once, Kirby saw something red. But it was just a ladybug.

The girl's mother came close to Kirby. She was sniffling. "My little girl has been sick. She needed something to cheer her up. The necklace made her happy. If only we could find it," she said.

Kirby broke into a cold sweat. The yellow stone! It was in his hand. He should have tossed it into the waterfall. He wanted to be done with it. But he heard the crying. And he forgot to throw it.

Now his hand tightened on it. Should he

rub it one more time? Was there *any* chance
it could do some good? Kirby didn't want to
rub the stone. But he did. And he wished
the child would find her necklace.

Kirby walked on. He stared into the
grass. Where could it be? And then he saw
something. It looked like glass. He bent
down. He grabbed a red necklace. "Is this
it?" he cried.

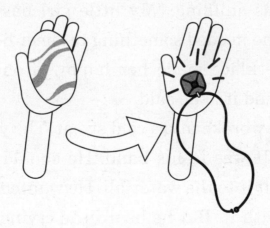

The mother and the little girl came
running.

"Oh, thank you! Thank you," the mother said.

"Yay!" screamed the little girl.

She hugged Kirby. He just stood there. He was shaken.

Mother and daughter left. Kirby tried to throw the yellow stone into the waterfall. Like he'd planned. But he couldn't.

8
WORRIED

Kirby headed home from school. It was raining. He wore his raincoat. He walked fast. Dad offered to drive him. But Kirby liked to walk, even in the rain.

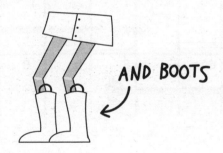

AND BOOTS

Kirby waited at Madison. It wasn't safe to cross yet. A tall boy stood beside him. He was tan. And he looked around Kirby's age.

But he looked tough. Kirby had never seen him before today.

The boy made Kirby nervous.

"What's your name?" the boy asked.

"Kirby Aki." Kirby stepped away. "Why? Who are you?"

"I'm looking for a kid like you. He was here this time last Monday," the boy said.

SU	M	TU	W	TH	F	SA
30	31 Saved a man	1	2	3	4	5
6	7	8	9	10	11	12

That was the day Kirby rescued the man. Eight days ago. Kirby was suddenly scared. Maybe this boy was the man's son. Maybe the man got hurt. He fell pretty hard. He didn't seem hurt. But maybe he was mad at Kirby. Kirby had made him fall.

"Did you see a rescue last week? A kid saved a man from being hit. A truck was coming. The kid saved him. The man had on a red shirt."

"No, I didn't see anything," Kirby said quickly. The light changed. He hurried across the street.

Kirby remembered the older lady. She'd seen the whole thing. She always wore a Dodgers cap. She knew Kirby. Knew his family. Kirby's mom helped her. She gave her rides to her appointments. She would tell the boy. That made Kirby nervous.

Kirby got home faster than usual. He needed to talk to his mom or dad. Mom was home.

"Mom, some tough-looking kid was at

the Madison light. He asked me about last Monday. Who pulled the man off the street? Did I see it? I'm scared. Maybe that man got hurt. You know. When he fell. Maybe he's coming after me. He didn't say he was hurt. He seemed okay but—"

DID HE
BREAK
HIS
FOOT?

"Honey," Mom said. "You saved his life. I'm sure he knows it. He would have gotten smashed. Been in the hospital. Or maybe even died. But the truck didn't hit him.

Because of you. You did something great. Surely he knows that."

"Yeah. But this kid *seemed* mean. He looked like the man I saved," Kirby said. "Well, kind of … Maybe."

"Calm down," Mom said. "Don't always look for the bad. That boy might have been the man's son. Maybe he just wants to find you. To thank you for saving his father. Maybe he wants to high-five you."

Kirby still looked worried.

Mom gave Kirby a hug. "Don't worry. I made another mince pie for tonight."

"That's great, Mom," Kirby said. "You are awesome. Thanks." But he was still worried.

9
ANOTHER B-MINUS?

Ms. Larimer returned the graded projects. Kirby knew he had done well. He liked learning about the okapi. He expected a B. He usually got B-minuses.

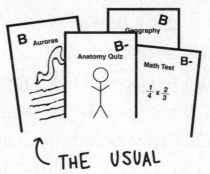

THE USUAL

Kirby thought Lee had done really well. He would get his usual A. The best project always got an award. Ms. Larimer liked doing that. The student got a special certificate. Lee would get it again. For sure.

NINE TIMES THIS YEAR!

CERTIFICATE OF EXCELLENCE

Yay!

Awarded to

Lee Watkins

Ms. Larimer

The projects were returned. Kirby peeked. Lee got a B. Wow, a B!

Lee was surprised. And a little angry. Kirby could tell he was not happy.

Would Kirby get a B? He wasn't so sure. Lee got a B. Kirby usually got a grade lower. So maybe he'd get a C-plus. Ms. Larimer was tough. But now? Maybe tougher than usual.

Ms. Larimer put his report down. Kirby

was almost afraid to look. But then he did. He gasped. There was a big red A on it. No way! Kirby was thrilled.

It was recess. Everybody was talking about their grades.

"I got a B-minus. That's good for me," Jalen said. "My folks will be happy. Heck, I'm happy! What'd you get, Kirby? You did better than me. You probably got a B-plus."

"I got an A," Kirby said. "It's my first A ever on a big project."

Jalen high-fived Kirby. "Good for you, dude. Your report was great. And cool. And funny too. I learned a lot about okapis."

Lee looked over at Kirby and Jalen. "What'd you guys get?" he asked.

"I got a B-minus. But Kirby got an A," Jalen said.

"That's crazy," Lee yelled. "You didn't mess up. Not like usual. But I did *way* better than you. It's impossible. How can you get an A? I only got a B. Let me see your report!"

The Okapi

A

Kirby showed Lee his report. There was the A. Big and red on the cover. And a note. *"Congratulations, Kirby. Yours was the best project in the class."*

Lee stared at Kirby. "That's not fair! You

know it's not. My report was better. It was the best. Everybody knows it. Everybody knows you're stupid, Kirby!"

Kirby's face turned warm. He was not the smartest kid in fourth grade. But he worked hard. He never got less than a B. So he wasn't stupid.

He thought his grade was fair. He did so much work. But what Lee said still hurt.

"Everybody knows you're stupid, Kirby!" Lee said again.

Some of the other kids laughed. But not all of them. Kirby's face got warmer. He was not the most popular kid in class. He had some good friends. But Lee had more friends.

Now Kirby felt terrible. Maybe he was a loser. Maybe the grade was a mistake. All the joy was gone. The excitement Kirby felt vanished.

10
CHANNEL 8

The next day there was a math test. Kirby felt sad. Lee had said mean things. Kirby almost got out the yellow stone. He almost made a wish. But he decided not to do that. No matter what.

The good things weren't because of the stone. He was tired of thinking about it.

He opened his math book. He studied hard. He did his homework.

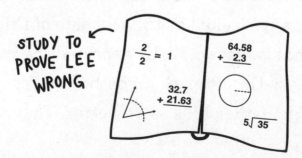

STUDY TO
PROVE LEE
WRONG

$\frac{2}{2} = 1$

$\begin{array}{r} 64.58 \\ + \ 2.3 \\ \hline \end{array}$

$\begin{array}{r} 32.7 \\ + 21.63 \\ \hline \end{array}$

$5 \overline{)\, 35}$

In the morning Kirby walked to school. He was still worried. What about the man in the red shirt? What if the man was hurt? Was he angry now? And looking for Kirby.

Kirby got to school. He didn't see the tough kid. He sighed with relief.

Ms. Larimer passed out the math tests. Kirby relaxed.

The problems looked familiar. Kirby quickly solved the first one. And then the second. He was done with the test first.

Kirby walked home from school. He kept looking around. Was anyone following him? Mom said Kirby saw the glass half empty. He always looked at the bad side of things.

That was true. Kirby expected the worst. Always. He often thought he wasn't good enough. Other kids were better. They were smarter. Cuter. Friendlier. More talented. Sometimes Kirby felt like a nobody.

Kirby neared his house. His parents waited for him in the front yard. He was surprised.

"Uh-oh," Kirby mumbled. "Trouble!"

Kirby saw a woman. She was getting out of a news van. It said Channel 8. She walked toward Kirby's parents. Mom and Dad were smiling.

"Kirby! This is Jessica Tate. From Channel 8," Mom cried.

Kirby was stunned. His father hugged him. His mother kissed him.

"What's happening?" Kirby asked.

"That man you saved? He wanted to find you. He looked for you. His kids did too. He told Channel 8 what you did. Jessica is here to interview you. For the Hero of the Month Award. You're going to be on TV," Dad said.

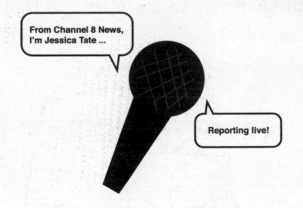

"No way!" Kirby cried.

"Oh yes way, honey," Mom said. "We are so proud of you!"

Kirby was interviewed. His parents were too. Jessica Tate told the story. About how Kirby saw a man in danger. About the speeding truck. About the yellow light.

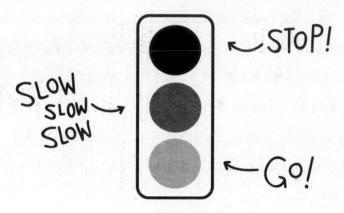

"This boy grabbed the man's shirt. He yanked him from the jaws of death," Jessica gushed.

The man who Kirby saved was there. So were his wife and kids. All four of them! Kirby recognized the oldest boy. The kid who had scared him. But the boy was smiling.

And friendly. The family hugged Kirby. Right there in the Akis' front yard.

Kirby saw Ms. Nealy. The lady with the Dodgers cap. She told Al who Kirby was.

"Kirby, you're Channel 8's Hero of the Month," Jessica said. "You are so brave. We are thrilled to give you this award."

Kirby shook Jessica's hand. He took the award. It read "Certificate of Honor." His parents beamed behind him. Al's family cheered.

AL'S FAMILY CHEER →

"One more thing, Kirby. Our sponsors

would like to reward you. This is a thousand-dollar savings bond. To thank you for your heroism."

Kirby was shocked. The award was great. But a thousand dollars? He loved it!

Jessica turned to the camera. "That's our hero, folks. What a shining example. This is Jessica Tate, reporting."

Kirby put his award in a special box. Then he gazed at his thousand-dollar savings bond. He put that in the box too. The only other item there was the yellow calcite. Al's yellow stone. The stone that brought good luck.

Kirby would never rub it again. But he would keep it forever. He'd learned to trust himself. He didn't need magic to believe.